WHAT
MOMMIES
DO BEST

WHAT MOMMIES DO BEST

BY **Laura Numeroff**

ILLUSTRATED BY **Lynn Munsinger**

SIMON & SCHUSTER BOOKS FOR YOUNG READERS
New York London Toronto Sydney Singapore

Mommies can teach you
how to ride a bicycle,

make a snowman with you,

and bake a delicious
cake for your birthday.

Mommies can help you
make a garden grow,

give you a
piggyback ride,

and take care of you
when you're sick.

Mommies can watch
the sun set with you,

sew the loose button
on your teddy bear,

and hold you when
you're feeling sad.

Mommies can take you
trick-or-treating,

help you give the
dog a bath,

and play with you
in the park.

Mommies can read you
a bedtime story,

tuck you in,

and kiss you good-night.

But best of all,
mommies can give you
lots and lots of love!